Rush
Montessori

For Aubert and his father
L.B.

For Michel and Laurence
rebels and co-conspirators
D.M.

MYRIAD BOOKS LIMITED
35 Bishopsthorpe Road, London SE26 4PA

First published in 2003 by
MIJADE PUBLICATIONS
16-18, rue de l'Ouvrage
5000 Namur-Belgium

© Laurence Bourguignon and Dominique Maes, 2003

Translation: Lisa Pritchard

ISBN 1 84746 037 2

Printed in China

Laurence Bourguignon & Dominique Maes

MAX

and the yellow tractor

MYRIAD BOOKS LIMITED

One spring morning, Max was up early.
The old jeep was still asleep when
Max left the barn.

Once out of the farmyard, Max turned left
towards the little wood. He loved it there.

The trees were full of birds, and he could hear the murmur of the little stream.

But today Max could hear another sound, a sort of roaring.
Something was coming round the bend…

It was a magnificent yellow tractor! He was much bigger than
Max, with huge wheels that made great clouds of dust. And he was
making really thick smoke. He beeped his horn and rushed past the
little red tractor at full speed.

That day, Max did lots of silly things. He got stuck in a rut.
He often started up his windscreen wipers by mistake.

He beeped for no reason, and made the cows run off in a panic.
Max was not thinking about his work.

That evening in the barn,
Max told the old jeep all about
meeting the big yellow tractor.
He was very excited!

"He's so strong, so fast! I'm going to zoom along like him and make
lots of thick smoke. We're going to be great friends, I just know it."

The old jeep coughed. "Be careful, Max," she said. "Don't forget
you're only a little tractor."

Max thought to himself, "She's jealous. Oh well, too bad. Anyway,
I've got a new friend now."

The next morning, Max went back to the little wood.

This time he didn't listen to the birds or the murmur of the stream.
He listened for the sound of a big
engine in the distance.

But he couldn't hear anything.
The big yellow tractor must
have gone somewhere else today.

All day, Max thought about the big yellow tractor
and tried to do everything just like him.

He drove fast. He made as much thick smoke as he could. He skidded on purpose so that he was covered in mud and dust.

On the way home, Max zoomed downhill, revving his engine like a racing car.

Suddenly Max caught sight of the old jeep.
She was coming up the hill and looking
a bit shaky.

"I'm going to give her a scare," he said to himself. He beeped as loud as he could and went even faster. Now she'd see what he could do!

But Max wasn't made to be a racer. His engine got too hot and steam came out from his bonnet. He had to stop and cool down.

The old jeep drove past, wheezing and creaking.
Max looked away. She was right, he was just a little tractor.
The big yellow tractor would never want to be friends
with him.

After that, Max got on with his work.
He drove carefully, and didn't do anything silly.
He didn't see the big yellow tractor and tried not to think about him.
Sometimes he listened, hoping to hear his engine rumbling in the distance.

One morning when he was coming
out of the woods, the farmer took
Max down a different track.

On either side of the track the wheat and the barley were nodding in the wind, like a sea of gold.

"The big yellow tractor did this," said Max, full of admiration.

Just then he caught sight of the big yellow tractor.

Max drove on and stopped beside him. He revved his engine gently but the big yellow tractor didn't reply. Max felt very small.

The farmer drove Max forward a little.
Then he got out and joined up
the two tractors.

Suddenly Max understood:
the big yellow tractor had broken down.
That had happened to him too, and another
tractor towed him back to the farm.

Was Max strong enough to tow the big yellow tractor?

Max pulled, and pulled… His wheels spun and his engine started to get hot, giving off really thick smoke. But he didn't have time to notice.

He gave an extra big heave and at last the big yellow tractor started to move.

Max was very proud to be towing him.

He drove carefully and slowly.
He didn't want anything to happen
to the big yellow tractor.

From time to time, he beeped
politely. He was very happy!

Max was exhausted when
he got home that evening.
But before he went to sleep
there was something he had to do.

The old jeep had not
said anything to Max for days.

"You were right," he said to her. "I'm just a silly little
tractor. But today I was a bit less silly, and I felt a little
bit bigger. Please can we be friends again? And tomorrow
I'll take you to meet my new friend."